Thi~ Lollipop and grandpa Book

longs to:

· ·

For my swimming buddy Roe, and all at Thame pool. PH

For Sandy and Charlie and all my pals at Ainslie Park. CJ

Lollipop and Grandpa Go Swimming

ISBN: 978-1-907912-13-9

Published in Great Britain by Phoenix Yard Books Ltd

This edition published 2012

Phoenix Yard Books
Phoenix Yard
65 King's Cross Road
London
WC1X 9LW

1 3 5 7 9 10 8 6 4 2

Book design by Insight Design Concepts

Printed in Singapore

A CIP catalogue record for this book is available from the British Library

www.phoenixyardbooks.com

Lollipop
and
Grandpa
Go Swimming

Penelope Harper
Illustrated by Cate James

Lollipop and Grandpa are going swimming.
Lollipop has a brand new swimsuit...

inflatable armbands that took
all of Grandpa's puff to blow up...

and the biggest towel Mum could
find, for drying off afterwards.

Lollipop peers out from the changing rooms.

The pool is very noisy with everyone
splashing and shouting, and splooshing
and whooping and having fun in the water.
Everyone, that is, except Lollipop.

Lollipop doesn't know how to swim.

Just when she thinks she might change her mind
and peel her swimming costume off again...

Grandpa takes her hand and whispers,
"Just a bit of water, Lollipop."

Grandpa is wearing a swimsuit that looks like it comes from a museum.
He has an ENORMOUS rubber ring around his middle,
AND armbands,
AND goggles,
AND flippers on his feet.

Like a giant frog, he SLIP-SLAPS
his way across the poolside.

SLIP-SLAP,
SLIP-SLAP,
SLIP-SLAP...

"Don't worry, Lollipop," says Grandpa,
"we're going to start off in the little pool.
In ten minutes, I'm sure you'll love it."

"First, floating!" says Grandpa, and he shows
Lollipop how to take her feet off the bottom
of the pool.

Lollipop finds it easy, but Grandpa keeps bobbing upside down.

"Next, we need to try some kicking," says Grandpa.

Lollipop does perfect little kicks, but Grandpa's flippers make huge splashing waves.

"Now, you need to learn how to hold your breath underwater."

Grandpa shows Lollipop how to take a big breath and then put her face into the water.
Lollipop thinks it's easy, but Grandpa forgets to stop talking when he puts his head under the water.

"Whoops!" he says. "That didn't taste very nice."

"Well, Lollipop, I do declare that you are
a natural swimmer," says Grandpa.

"Am I ready to explore the big pool?" asks Lollipop.

"Of course you are!" cries Grandpa.
"We're intrepid deep-sea divers and
there's sunken treasure to be found."

The big pool still seems ENORMOUS.

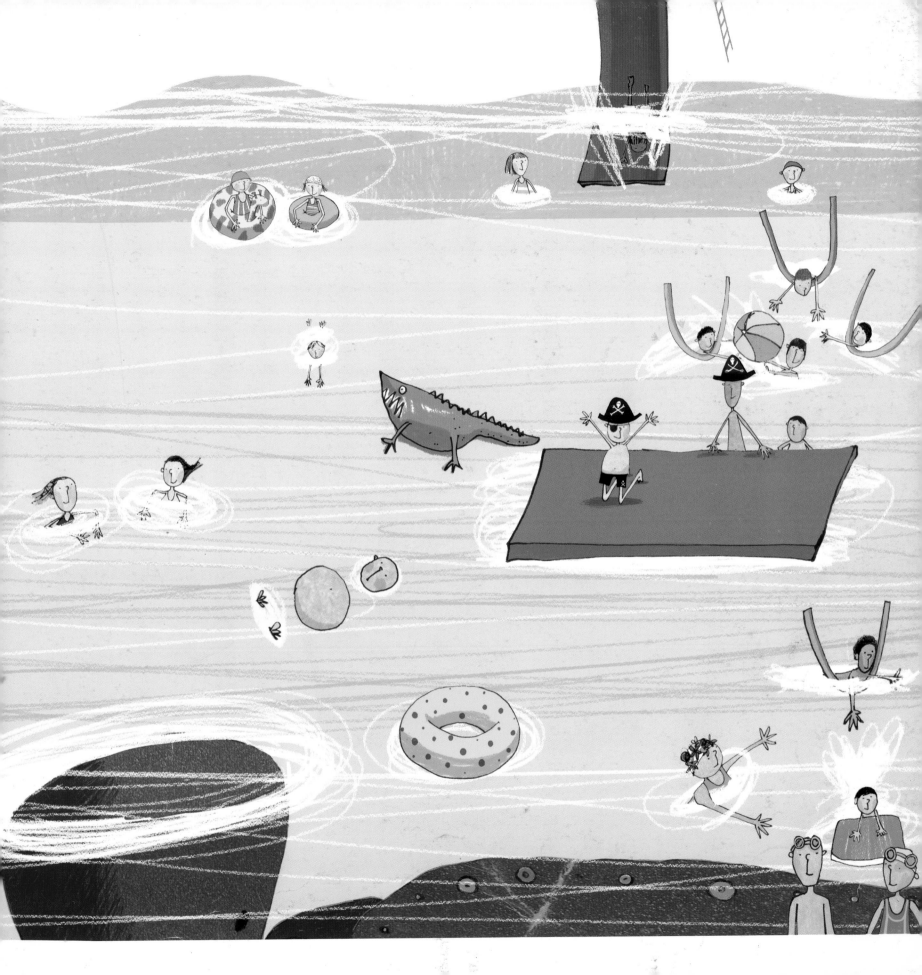

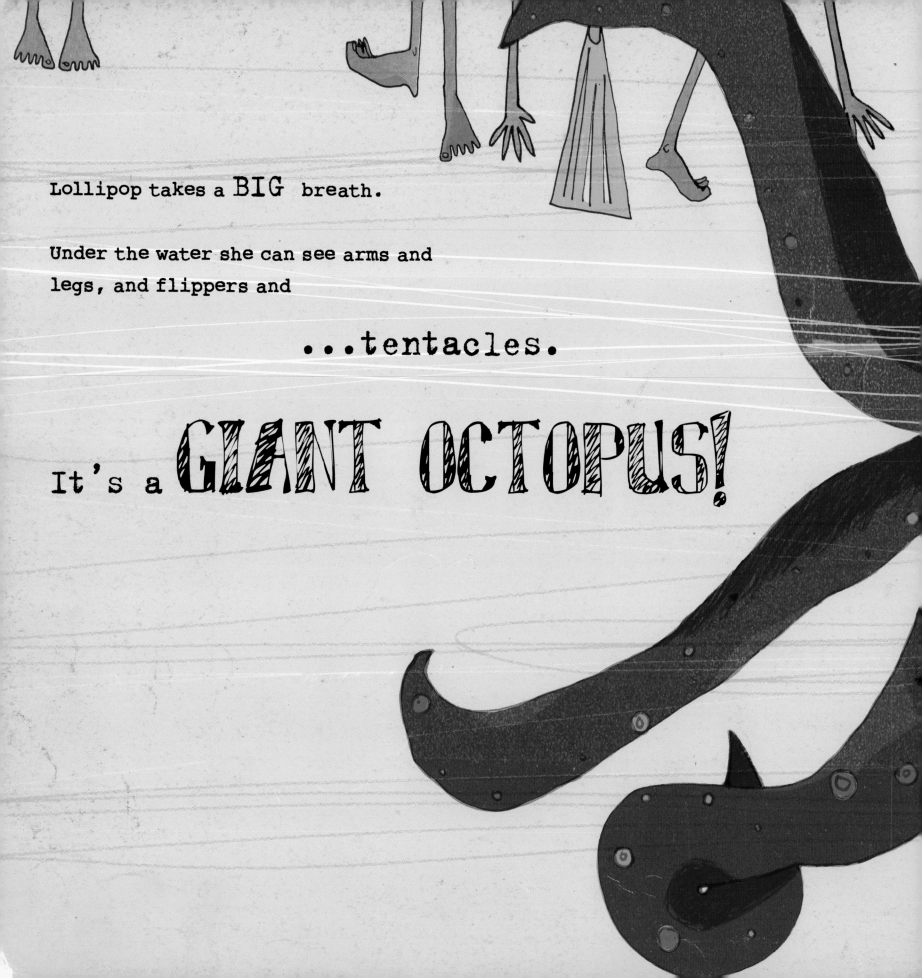

Lollipop takes a BIG breath.

Under the water she can see arms and legs, and flippers and

...tentacles.

It's a GIANT OCTOPUS!

Lollipop lets out an underwater yelp.
"Bobble-obble-obble-obble-obble!"

Lollipop wrestles with the
GIANT OCTOPUS,
and he soon decides that
she's too much bother
to try and eat.

"That was so close, Grandpa," Lollipop gasps.
But it isn't long before they spot something else in their path.
"G - G - G - Grandpa..."
gulps Lollipop.

Emerging from the dark waters of the
deep end is a knee-wobbling, jaw-dropping,
tummy-fluttering, absolutely
GINORMOUS,

"WOW!" cries Lollipop.
"It's the biggest mammal on the planet!
They told us that at the Natural History Museum."

It's too ginormous to swim around, so Lollipop
and Grandpa decide to climb on top of it.

"You'd better hold onto your armbands, Lollipop!"
shouts Grandpa.

"She's going to **BLOW!**"

WHOOOOOOOOOOOSH!

The big blue whale shoots them straight out of her blowhole.

Up and up and up, then down and down and down they go with the gushing water, until...

SPLA-DOOOOOSSHHH!

As the bubbles clear, suddenly Lollipop sees...

THE SUNKEN TREASURE!

Grandpa dives down to the bottom to reach the gold rings,
then he and Lollipop climb out of the pool.

"We've found it, we've found it!
I can't believe it!" shouts Lollipop.
She and Grandpa do a victory dance.

They're just about to count their
gold when...

"Stop right there!"

"UH-OH!"

"**Aaaaaar!** Whoever tries to steal our gold
must walk our plank!" says one of the pirates.

"Oh no!" thinks Lollipop.
"The plank is over the deep end,
and I'm too little to swim in there."

"Step aside, Lollipop," says Grandpa, hitching up his rubber ring and adjusting his goggles.

Grandpa SLIP-SLAPS his way to the plank at the deep end.

Suddenly, the lifeguard blows his whistle.

PEEEEEEEEEEEEEEEEEEEEEEEEP!

He orders the pirates out of the swimming pool.

Their mums look very cross.

Lollipop spots an arm, waving from the water.

It's Grandpa!
"HOORAY!" cheers Lollipop.

Grandpa swims over to the side and says,
"I'm pooped, Lollipop. Perhaps we'd better go home for a cup of tea."

"Maybe," says Lollipop. "Or we could just stay ten more minutes."